Disney Adventures

②

CASEBUSTERS

The Legend of Deadman's Mine

By Joan Lowery Nixon

Disney PRESS

New York

With love to Timothy William Quinlan — J.L.N.

Printed in the United States of America.

1 3 5 7 9 10 8 6 4 2

Library of Congress Catalog Card Number: 94-71791
ISBN: 0-7868-3047-6 (trade)/0-7868-4019-6 (pbk.)

1

SHORTLY AFTER their arrival at the Austin Dude Ranch, Brian and Sean Quinn stopped at the door of cabin A to glance down the hill. At the foot of the hill was a swimming pool, its water skimmed with gold in the late afternoon sunlight.

Between the pool and the forest, a meadow stretched like a soft green blanket, broken only by a large campfire pit ringed with split-log benches.

Nine-year-old Sean began to picture a roaring campfire . . . hot dogs . . . toasted marshmallows. . . . He licked his lips.

"Come on," Brian said. "We've got to show up

at the lodge for Mr. Austin's meeting in less than half an hour."

Once inside the cabin, they dumped their suitcases on their bunks. Brian and Sean smiled as they glanced around at the plain wooden walls and the floors decorated only with woven rag rugs. The Austin Dude Ranch looked just the way they thought a dude ranch ought to look.

Brian took a deep breath. "Smell that cool mountain air," he said.

Sean took a couple of sniffs. "It smells like horses to me," he answered.

Brian made a face at Sean. "A dude ranch is supposed to smell like horses."

"Do you think they'll let us go for a ride right away?" Sean asked. Riding horses was what Sean had been looking forward to most.

"They have to show you how to do it first," Brian told him laughingly. "You've never even been on a horse."

"Yeah?" countered Sean. "Well, neither

have you!"

Just then a wiry, tanned boy, almost as tall as Brian, bounced into the cabin.

"They'll talk about camp schedules at the first meeting," the boy said. "Then you'll know what's going on. Oh, and you should know that I'm Carter Burton III."

"Hi," Brian said. "I'm—"

"I know who you are," Carter said. "I read Hank's roster. You're Brian Quinn. You're thirteen, and you're from a dinky little town called Redbud or something."

Sean glared at Carter. "That's Redoaks, California," he corrected. "And it's not a dinky little town. It's a real neat place to live."

Carter shrugged, muttered a "Whatever," and resumed talking to Brian. "And you came with your dinky little brother, Vaughn."

"That's Sean! And I'm not dinky, either."

"This is my third trip to Hank Austin's dude ranch," Carter explained to Brian, ignoring Sean.

"I know all about the place, so if you have any questions, just ask me."

Carter flopped onto Sean's bunk, pulled a handful of peanuts out of his pocket, and began to pop them open.

"Hey!" Sean said as Carter began dropping the shells on the floor. "Quit making a mess."

"It's on your side. You clean it up," Carter said. He smirked. "You better clean it up or you'll get in trouble when the cabins are inspected."

Sean's face grew red as his temper began to flare, but Brian put a restraining hand on his arm.

"Come on," he told Sean as he scooped up the shells and dropped them into a nearby wastepaper basket. "Let's go to the lodge. Mr. Austin told us to get our stuff stowed away, then meet in the lodge."

Sean pointed at the wooden chests at the foot of their bunks. "I guess we're supposed to put our clothes and stuff in these." He flipped open the lid, unzipped his suitcase, and dumped the contents into the chest.

"There," Sean said. "All unpacked."

Brian was neatly arranging his clothes.

"Hurry up," Carter said impatiently. "It's time to go." He left the cabin and started up the path toward the lodge. Sean and Brian scrambled to catch up with him.

"Can we ask Mr. Austin when he'll let us ride the horses?" Sean asked.

"It better be soon," Carter said, "before they all get stolen."

"Stolen?" Brian asked. "What are you talking about?"

"I'm talking about horse thieves," Carter said.

Brian was so startled that he stumbled over a rock in the path. "Are you saying that someone's stealing Mr. Austin's horses?" he asked.

"The horse thieves haven't got to Hank's horses yet," Carter said, "but they probably will. Over on the nearest working ranch—where Wade Morrison breeds and sells horses—a valuable breeding stallion named Nightstar was stolen just last week and disappeared without a clue. The sheriff was here, asking questions, and so were a couple of newspaper reporters. You probably never heard of Nightstar, but he was a winning racehorse."

"Was?" asked Brian.

"He was retired five years ago," Carter said.

"What makes you think the thief who stole Nightstar would be after Mr. Austin's horses?" Brian asked. "A dude ranch isn't a place for valuable racehorses."

Sean grinned. "I don't think Chandler here knows as much about horses as he thinks."

Carter turned to Sean. "That's Carter," he grumbled, "and I know a lot more about horses than you do . . . Vaughn."

When Carter began lecturing Brian about horses, Sean decided he'd had enough of Carter Burton III and ran on ahead. He was the first to reach the steps leading off the lodge porch, where a ranch hand was sitting in a battered oak rocking chair, rubbing strips of leather with a stained rag. His heavily wrinkled face was as deeply tanned as the leather.

Sean introduced himself. "Hi. I'm Sean Quinn."

"I'm called Woody." He smiled at Sean.

"What are you doing?" asked Sean as he leaned closer to watch.

"Cleaning a harness."

"Cool," Sean said. He imagined putting the harness on one of the horses, then climbing up into the saddle. He couldn't wait for his first ride.

Brian was asking Carter a question when they clumped up the wooden stairs to the porch.

"That horse you said was stolen," he suggested. "If it was taken out of the barn in a truck or a horse trailer, wouldn't somebody have heard something?"

"How should I know?" Carter said, shrugging.

"Woody," Sean said, "this is my brother, Brian." Brian and Woody exchanged hellos.

"Hey, Brian, maybe Woody can answer your

question," Sean said.

"Right!" Brian said, brightening. "Carter and I were talking about the horse theft," he explained, "and there are lots of things I want to know." From force of habit, Brian pulled out a pen and a notebook from his jeans pocket. "Did the sheriff check to see if anyone had spotted a horse trailer on the highway at night?" Brian began. "And did he look around for hoofprints, in case the horse was led away on foot?"

Woody shrugged. "Don't ask me," he said, directing his attention to the harness. "That's Wade Morrison's business." He looked up at Brian and squinted. "I don't mind anybody's business but my own."

"But do you happen to know if they found anything unusual around the stables or the grounds?"

"A criminal not only takes away something from the scene of a crime," Sean said. "He also leaves something—maybe just a clump of dirt from his shoe or a blade of grass."

It was one of the first rules of investigating, something he'd heard his father mention a million times.

"What's with you two dorks?" Carter snapped. "You ask so many questions someone might think you're private investigators or something."

"Our dad is a private investigator," Brian said. "And someday I plan to be one, too. This case of a disappearing horse interests me."

"If I were you," Woody said, "I'd stop trying to play detective about that missing black stallion. Sooner or later the sheriff will find the horse." He looked sharply at Brian. "Mind your own business, like I do, and you won't get into any trouble or cause any trouble."

Brian sighed and reluctantly tucked his notebook and pen back into his pocket.

Sean, however, was glad. He always enjoyed working with Brian on their investigations, but this was a vacation, and he didn't want to do any investigating.

"I'm getting hungry," Sean said. "I wonder if

we'll have a campfire and a cookout tonight."

"We'll have a campfire," Carter said. He looked down at Sean and sneered. "But it might be too scary for a little kid like you, because Hank is going to tell ghost stories."

He pulled another handful of peanuts out of his pocket and began munching.

"I'm not afraid of ghosts!" Sean insisted. "I even helped our dad and Brian uncover some so-called ghosts that were haunting guests at a place called the Pine Tree Inn." He wished that what he'd said about not believing in ghosts were true. But the truth was, he did believe in ghosts.

"Yeah?" Carter asked. He didn't look impressed. In fact, his eyes sparkled as though he knew a good joke. "If that's so," he said in a challenging tone, "then maybe you won't mind running into the ghost of a crazy old prospector who lost his silver mine and sometimes wanders through the mountains around here."

"A crazy old prospector? Oh, sure," Brian said skeptically.

"The story's true," Carter insisted. "Isn't it, Woody?"

"Yep," Woody said. "I've even seen the ghost once myself."

Brian couldn't believe it! He was just about to ask Woody a question when he saw the ranch hand point at the pile of peanut shells at Carter's feet.

"Carter," he barked, "I told you before to stop littering! You know the rules. Now pick up those shells."

Carter heaved a huge sigh and began to pick up the shells.

Ordinarily, Sean would have enjoyed teasing Carter about having to pick up the peanut shells, but he couldn't help thinking about what Woody had said about the prospector's ghost.

He glanced out at the rolling grassland and the

dark woods just beyond. In the daylight the dude ranch didn't seem the least bit scary. Sean shivered. Ghosts never came out during the day, but what might happen at night?

2

As Brian, Sean, and Carter entered the main room of the lodge, Hank Austin, the owner of the ranch, shouted to them over the loud babble of the other campers.

"Come on inside, boys, and find yourselves seats."

The lodge was decorated with wagon-wheel chandeliers, deep sofas and chairs draped with Indian blankets, and wood carvings of horses that stood on most of the tables.

Brian, Sean, and Carter took the nearest available chairs, and Mr. Austin pounded on a table until the other boys quieted down to listen.

"There are a few things to go over before supper," Mr. Austin began. He explained to the boys that there were rules for making beds, sweeping cabin floors, being good bunkmates, and strictly following safety regulations.

"Other than that," Mr. Austin said, "you boys are here to have fun. Now, we've got an early ride planned for tomorrow morning with a breakfast cookout down by the creek."

"Yahoo!" Sean yelled.

Carter snorted. "He hasn't even been here one day and he thinks he's a cowboy already," he muttered.

"Remember," Mr. Austin said, "we use a buddy system. No one is to take off in the woods on his own. Understood?"

He looked right at Carter as he said, "It's too easy to get lost."

Sean grinned when he saw the embarrassed look on Carter's face. "So you were dumb enough to get lost," he whispered to Carter. "I bet that's a good story. Maybe Woody will tell us about it if you don't."

The husky boy to Sean's left chuckled. "I want to hear that story, too," he said.

Carter shot them both an angry glance, then jumped up and sat down at a table across the room.

"Hi, I'm Mike Dennis," the husky boy said to Sean.

"I'm Sean Quinn."

Mike lowered his voice and said, "I'm in the same cabin as you, so I have to put up with Carter the dweeb, too."

"He's a real jerk. What's with him?"

Mike made a face. "My mom knows Carter's mom. I'm supposed to try to understand Carter and be nice to him because his mom's always getting married and that makes him feel mixed up and . . ."

"Did you say, 'always getting married'?" Sean clapped a hand over his mouth as Brian turned to frown at him.

"Well, four times, anyway," Mike whispered.

Mr. Austin pounded on the table again and spoke to Sean and Mike. "Pay attention now, boys," he said, and introduced his wife, Rose. Mrs. Austin explained that she'd always be on hand to answer questions, take care of cuts and scrapes, make sure letters were written to parents, and help anyone who might feel a little homesick.

Sean thought she looked friendly. She even reminded him of his favorite teacher back at Redoaks Elementary School.

Brian nudged Sean when Mrs. Austin mentioned "homesick." The two brothers grinned at each other. Homesick? they both thought. No way. They'd see their parents in two weeks, which would be soon enough. Living on a real dude ranch was going to be a great adventure.

"I want you to meet Cookie, the ranch's cook," Mr. Austin said. "Cookie has some rules of his own you'll need to follow."

A weathered, wrinkled, bowlegged man stepped to Mr. Austin's side. Sean couldn't help grinning.

The man's scraggly tufts of white hair looked as though someone had run over his head with a dull lawn mower.

"Mr. Austin feeds his guests well," Cookie growled, "so I know there won't be any complaints about my cooking. There'll be no food fights, and if you want dessert, you'll eat your vegetables."

"He's just like my mom," Mike mumbled to Sean.

Imagining a mother who looked like Cookie was too much for Sean. He burst out laughing.

Cookie's stare pinned Sean to his chair. "Son," he barked, "is there something about vegetables you find funny?"

"No, sir," squeaked Sean. "I like vegetables."

"Good," Cookie said, "because I'm thinking of cooking up a mess of turnip greens special for you tonight."

Sean gulped. "Yes, sir," he said.

Just then Cookie winked at Sean. Mr. Austin

laughed and clapped Cookie on the shoulder. "No turnip greens tonight," he said. "Cookie's already planned a real cowboy supper of grilled steak and baked beans to start you off on your two weeks as dude-ranch hands."

The boys broke into a loud cheer. Sean smiled at Cookie. He was thankful he hadn't started his two-week adventure by getting into trouble. Besides, turnip greens sounded awful!

After the meeting, Brian and Sean introduced themselves to their bunkmates. Besides Mike Dennis, who was ten years old and said all he really liked was football, they met fourteen-year-old Dan Page and Bobby Wilson, who had just turned eight.

"My favorite team is the Cowboys," Mike explained. "But I also like the Rams."

Dan shook his head. "The Rams stink." He looked at Brian. "What about you?"

Brian shrugged. "I'm not much of a football fan, really," he said.

Dan smiled. "Me, neither. Maybe I should be. It would make my parents happy. They complain that I spend too much time with my computer. In fact, they sent me to this dude ranch just to separate me from my computer and make sure I get plenty of fresh air and exercise."

"You're good with computers?" Brian asked. "Cool!" He had an idea. "I wonder if there's a computer on the ranch."

"I know there is," Dan said, then frowned. "The only problem is I had to promise my parents I wouldn't touch a keyboard the entire time I was here."

Just then Mr. Austin walked past, and Brian immediately ran to catch up with him.

"Mr. Austin," Brian asked, "would you mind if I ask you some questions?"

"Sure thing," Mr. Austin said. "That's why I'm here." He gave Brian a big smile. "The fact is, though, I thought I'd covered everything you'd need to know." He scratched his head. "I did mention the pool hours, didn't I?"

"My questions aren't about your dude ranch," Brian explained.

Mr. Austin gave Brian a puzzled, sideways glance. "They're not?" he said.

"No," Brian said. "They're about the missing horse—Nightstar."

Mr. Austin looked meaningfully at Brian. "Now how in the world would you know about Nightstar?" he asked.

"That's the thing," said Brian. "I don't know much more than that he was stolen."

Brian could tell from Mr. Austin's confused expression that he still didn't understand.

"My dad's a private investigator," explained Brian. "Someday I'd like to be one, too, and this case interests me."

Mr. Austin nodded, then looked at his watch. "We've got a few minutes," he said, "but I don't know if I'll have the answers you're looking for."

Great! Brian thought as he whipped out his

notebook. He got right to work. "If the horse was taken out of the barn in a truck or a horse trailer," he began, "wouldn't somebody have heard something?"

"As Wade Morrison told me," Mr. Austin said, "most of the ranch hands had driven into Reno to a dance and didn't get back until around one in the morning. At the estimated time of the theft, Morrison was at home, along with a couple of hands who stayed in the bunkhouse, but they all claimed they slept soundly and didn't hear a thing."

"Did they check for hoofprints," Brian asked, "in case the horse was led away on foot?"

"As a matter of fact," Mr. Austin said, "they did. But I guess the ground around the stables had been raked. There were no prints at all."

Brian made notes as fast as he could. Then he had a thought. "According to the map my dad showed us before we came here," he said, drumming his pen on his notebook, "there's only one road out of here. It's the one that connects with the highway to Reno. Did the sheriff check to see if anyone spotted a horse trailer on the highway that night?"

Mr. Austin shook his head in disbelief. "I do declare, son," he said, grinning, "if I didn't know better, I'd say you already were a professional private investigator."

"Thanks," Brian said. "Well?"

"Well what?" Mr. Austin asked, then remembered. "Oh, right. He checked, but nobody had."

A gong sounded. "That's the call to dinner," Mr. Austin said. "Did we take care of all your questions?"

"For now," Brian said, flipping his notebook closed. "Thanks."

Mr. Austin nodded, then turned to address the campers. "The tables are outside, boys, and it's cafeteria style. Help yourselves." He had to quickly step out of the way as two dozen hungry campers stampeded through the main doors of the lodge.

"Come on, Brian," Sean called out excitedly, "before I starve to death."

"Wait for me!" Bobby yelled as he ran after Sean.

THE BOYS HAD PILED THEIR PLATES high with food and were climbing over one another looking for places to sit.

Sean was seated at a table with his fork halfway to his mouth, dreaming about how good the food was going to taste, when he saw Bobby standing alone looking for an empty seat. Sean thought he looked so miserable he might cry. Sean sighed, put down his fork, and walked over. "Since we're going to be bunkmates," he told Bobby, "come on and sit with us."

Bobby beamed. He looked so grateful, in fact, that he reminded Sean of a puppy that begged to be picked up. He tagged after Sean, right on his heels, and squeezed in on the bench next to him.

The boys wolfed down their food and became so excited talking about what the dude ranch was going to be like that they were surprised to discover it was already getting dark.

At the bottom of the hill, Mr. Austin had built a large campfire, and it blazed high with a whoosh and a crackle. All at once the boys scrambled down the hill and found places to sit on the split-log benches that ringed the campfire. A few of the ranch hands, including Woody and Cookie, sat with them.

"S'mores for dessert," Mr. Austin said, and passed around long sticks and marshmallows to toast. "It just so happens I know a ghost story."

It was a story Sean had heard before from Sam Miyako, Brian's best friend. Sam had earned a reputation back in their neighborhood as someone who was always trying to frighten the younger kids with scary stories. Sean was Sam's favorite target.

The story was about a ghost who kept following people, crying, "Give me my bones!" And even though Sean already knew the story, it still seemed awfully scary outside in the dark.

Suddenly in the distance there was a mournful howling.

"It's the prospector's ghost!" Carter said ominously.

"For goodness' sake, Carter," Mr. Austin said, "that was just a coyote. Don't worry about coyotes," he told the boys. "They don't want to meet up with you any more than you want to meet up with them."

Carter spoke up. "Tell them about the lost mine and the ghost of the prospector who protects it."

"A lost mine?" asked Brian.

"Is it somewhere on this ranch?" Mike asked. The boys began to fidget excitedly.

"The lost mine is a legend," Mr. Austin said. "And so is the prospector's ghost. They're just stories that got out of hand."

"But there were directions to the mine," Carter said. "I heard about them."

Cookie chuckled. "Sure there were. And they were so confusing it's no wonder the prospector got lost."

"What were they?" asked Brian.

Cookie frowned, trying to remember. "Supposedly there was something about finding the highest peak and following the trail to a tree with two tops," he said. "From there it was downhill to a rock ledge, and facing south, or something like that."

"It does sound confusing," Brian said.

"I bet I could follow that trail," Carter said. "Just because the lost mine hasn't been found doesn't mean it isn't there. In fact, I think I have a pretty good idea just where it is."

Mike nudged Sean. "Carter's a real pain. He pretends he knows everything. I guess he can't stand it if somebody else gets more attention than he does."

"Now listen carefully, boys," Mr. Austin said firmly, his eyes coming to rest on Carter. "Don't get any ideas about hunting for a lost mine. There are abandoned mines all over Nevada. But none of them are haunted, and all of them could be extremely dangerous." He glanced around the campfire meaningfully. "The story's just make-believe. But even if the mine did exist, it would be hazardous. Those old shafts are nothing but rotten timbers and narrow passageways, and cave-ins are a real possibility. I want to return you to your parents safe and sound."

"I'd still like to hear the story," Sean said. "Will you tell us? Please?"

"As long as you keep in mind it's only a story," Mr. Austin said, relenting. The boys all agreed, and Mr. Austin began. "There was a lot of silver mining in Nevada back in the 1800s," he explained, "but when the United States passed the Coinage Act of 1873, the silver dollar was omitted from the official currency. So," he said, "when the government stopped making silver dollars it caused the price of silver to drop, and most of the mines closed down." He paused, staring into the fire. "Well," he continued finally, "some of those mines contained fine veins of silver, but with prices so low it would have cost more than it was worth to try to mine the ore."

He pointed off into the distance. "There was supposed to be one mine in particular near-abouts that had produced an especially top grade of silver." His eyes roamed slowly to one side, then the other. "But there were some . . . accidents in the mine. Terrible, horrifying accidents," he said, shaking his head.

"Ever since, that mine has been known as . . . Deadman's Mine."

There was some restless murmuring from the boys.

"Around 1890," Mr. Austin said, "an old prospector won the deed to the mine in a poker game and set out to work it, sure that the price of silver would soon return to what it had been."

"Only he couldn't find the mine," Carter finished in a dramatic tone of voice.

"What happened to the prospector?" Brian asked.

Mr. Austin paused for a moment. "No one knows. He wandered off into the mountains . . . and disappeared."

Sean gulped.

"Nobody ever saw him again?" Mike asked, his voice squeaking.

Mr. Austin slowly shook his head. "Legend says that late at night his ghost wanders through the ranch to frighten folks away from looking for his mine."

"His ghost wanders, all right," Woody said suddenly. "But that's not all. To keep people from snooping around looking for his mine, he's put brush in front of the doorway to hide it. And his skeleton is standing guard just inside the entrance to scare away trespassers."

He paused and gave Brian and Sean a chilling stare. "Mr. Austin's right," he said. "Looking for mines could be downright dangerous in more ways than one. Coming upon a skeleton is one thing," he warned them, "but coming up face-to-face with an angry ghost could cause you a heap of trouble!"

3

LATER THAT NIGHT, as the boys got ready for bed, Mike teased Carter about the time he got lost looking for Deadman's Mine.

"I didn't get lost," Carter snapped. "I was trying to follow Woody."

"What for?" Brian asked.

"He knows where the mine is. I'm sure he does."

"Mr. Austin said Deadman's Mine is just a story," Sean said.

Carter smiled. "That's what he wants you to think. But the mine exists, all right. And I'll prove it."

"Even if the mine exists," Brian said, sitting down on his bed, "what makes you think that Woody knows where it is?"

"Because he knows things about the mine that aren't in other people's stories when they tell the legend," Carter explained. "Like the skeleton guarding the entrance and the pile of brush hiding the doorway."

Brian pulled out his notebook and began scribbling.

"Don't you even think about trying to find the mine!" Carter yelled. "I was here first, and I'm going to find it! Not you!"

Sean had heard enough from Carter Burton III. "My brother is ten times better at this than you are," he said. "And I bet he could find the lost mine faster than you."

"Oh yeah?" said Carter.

"Yeah," said Sean.

"Hey, you guys," Brian said. "Remember what Mr. Austin said. Looking for the lost mine could be dangerous."

"I'm not afraid," Carter said huffily. "Just you watch. I'll find that mine."

*   *   *

SEAN LAY ON HIS BED in a pool of soft moonlight that sifted through the window. He tried unsuccessfully to fall asleep. He was thinking about Carter. And Bobby. Bobby had stuck to Sean all day like a piece of gum on his shoe. He had even insisted on claiming the bunk next to Sean's.

Oh well, Sean thought, when Bobby gets to know some of the other kids he'll stop hanging on to me. Until then Sean decided he could put up with a tagalong. But what could he do about Carter?

He listened to the far-off cry of a coyote. Suddenly he tensed when he heard the soft tread of what sounded like footsteps on the gravel outside the cabin.

"Brian," Sean whispered urgently, "are you still awake?"

"Yes," Brian whispered back. He was lying on his back with his hands crossed under his head. "I've been thinking about that stolen horse. Have you?"

"Nope," Sean said. "I've been wondering about that prospector. Do ghosts make sounds when they walk? I mean, can you hear their footsteps?"

"No and no," Brian answered.

"Then that probably wasn't the prospector's ghost wandering past our cabin a few minutes ago."

"No way," said Brian. "It was probably just one of the ranch hands."

"Be quiet. Go to sleep," Mike mumbled from under his blanket, and for a few moments all Sean could hear was a snuffling kind of snore from Dan's bunk and a rhythmic whistle from Bobby's.

Sean began to relax. His brother was right, he decided. "Good night," Sean whispered to Brian. But when he got no answer Sean figured that Brian had fallen asleep.

Brian's whisper startled Sean. "The first thing to ask ourselves is, Why?"

"Huh?" Sean mumbled. "Why what?"

"Why the horse was stolen." Brian rolled onto

his side, propped up on one elbow. "Dad always considers the motive—the reason for doing something. If we knew what the motive was, we ought to be able to figure out who stole the horse."

From under his blanket Sean smothered a loud yawn. "Carter said the horse was expensive. So who'd get the most out of stealing him?"

Brian thought for a minute. "What if the horse wasn't taken off this part of the mountain?" he asked.

"What are you talking about, Brian?"

"If no one saw a horse trailer on the highway that night, then that could mean the horse was walked or ridden away and hidden somewhere near here."

"Where?" Sean asked. "In someone's barn? The horse would be discovered near here."

"It wouldn't have to be a real barn. It could be anyplace that could keep the horse comfortable and dry."

"Why wouldn't the thief take the horse as far

away from here as he could?" Sean asked.

"The police would ask if anyone had seen a horse trailer at night, and somebody might have. But if the thief waited until everyone was sure the horse had been taken far away, he could move the horse in a trailer in broad daylight and no one would pay any attention."

"Okay, okay," Sean conceded, suddenly too tired to give much thought to Brian's theories. "Whatever you say."

"If the horse is stashed around here," Brian said, "I bet we could find him."

Sean groaned. "Brian," he said, "I want to ride horses and learn how to rope cattle and go on cookouts and swim in the swimming pool. The last thing I want to do is go searching for a stolen horse."

"Nightstar," Brian informed him.

"Whoever," Sean sighed. He knew his brother well enough to know that once Brian became interested in a case, nothing could distract him.

"Let's talk about it more tomorrow," Sean said. "Now go to sleep," he muttered, and rolled onto his side, away from Brian.

There was enough moonlight in the room so Sean could see, across the room, that Carter was wide awake and watching him.

Snoop! Sean thought. Carter probably had been awake all this time listening to what he and Brian had been saying.

Sean pulled his blanket up to his chin, closed his eyes, and tried to sleep. But he couldn't. Instead he kept thinking about the prospector's ghost. And about Carter Burton III. The worst part was that Sean couldn't decide which was worse.

A LOUD KNOCK on the cabin door woke Sean with a start. "Help!" he yelled as he tumbled out of bed and onto the floor.

Carter laughed and sat up. "That was just Woody waking everyone up. Better get used to it. It'll happen every morning."

"How can it be morning?" Bobby complained. "It's still dark."

Carter got up and flipped on the light switch, and the two bare bulbs that hung from the ceiling instantly flooded the room in a blinding glare.

From under a pile of blankets Mike groaned and rubbed his eyes. "What happens if we don't get up?" he asked. "They aren't going to arrest us or anything like that."

But Brian was already up and pulling on his clothes. "If you don't get up, you'll miss the breakfast cookout," he reminded them. "Remember what Cookie told us to expect. There will be sizzling bacon and hash brown potatoes and scrambled eggs and biscuits and jam and . . ."

"And a trail ride!" Sean grabbed for his shirt and jeans. He was suddenly so eager for the day's activities to begin that he forgot about his worries the night before.

Bobby was the last to finish dressing. "Wait for me!" he shouted as he hurriedly tugged on his jacket. He ran to catch up with Sean, and they all followed Carter to the stables, where everyone had been told to meet.

The eastern sky was streaked with early light, pale pink against an outline of thin white clouds. A row of horses—black, white, brown, spotted, and gray—had already been saddled and were hitched to the top rail of the fence that stretched in front of the stables. The horses bobbed their heads up and down, and their warm breath created steam clouds in the cool air.

Sean ran excitedly from horse to horse. "I wonder which one will be mine," he called to Brian. Sean reached out to stroke the nose of a spotted horse, but the horse snorted so loudly that Sean jumped back.

Woody stepped up beside him. "Come on, cowboy," he said to Sean. "I'll show you how to mount your horse. Climb up here on the block.

"Riders never walk close behind a horse," Woody said loudly, for the benefit of all the campers. "And they always mount from the left side, putting their left foot into the stirrups and throwing their right leg over their saddles.

"Never start out until your stirrups are adjusted to fit and you're sitting comfortably," he explained. "Hold the reins firmly. Show the horse that you're in charge. Pull on the right rein to turn the horse's head toward the right, and pull on the left rein if you want to turn left.

"Stay with the group," Woody cautioned, "and never kick a horse to make him run. Some light pressure from your knees is plenty."

The horses became impatient and began snuffling and stamping. Sean reached down to pat the neck of his horse. "Easy, boy," he said gently. In a movie he'd seen on television, he'd heard a cowboy talk to his horse like that.

The spotted horse seemed to understand, giving a last bob of his head before quieting. Sean felt proud of himself until he heard Carter snicker.

"Don't call your horse 'boy.' You're riding a filly, and her name is Goldie."

Mr. Austin mounted a tall, reddish brown bay and raised a hand. "Let's go," he said.

One by one the horses obediently fell into line.

"Oh my gosh," Sean told himself as his horse started forward. He took a deep breath and held tightly to the reins. It was awkward sitting in the saddle at first. But as his horse fell into a steady stride, Sean began to relax. Wow, he thought to himself, this is really fun.

By the time the group turned off the trail and headed for the breakfast area next to a creek, the sun was bright and warm and not a cloud was left in the sky.

The smell of crisp bacon and flapjacks on the outdoor grill was so enticing that Sean could hardly wait until one of the ranch hands took Goldie's reins. He eagerly climbed down and ran to join the other boys who had already lined up, plates and forks in hand.

Sean looked around nervously for Bobby and sighed with relief when he saw him off talking with two other boys from another cabin. Bobby was a nice enough kid, Sean decided, but Sean needed some breathing space. He found a seat on a split-log bench a little distance from the rest of the group and began to eat.

Brian sat down next to Sean and glanced carefully to both sides. "Have you thought about what I said last night?" he asked Sean.

As his jaws worked slowly up and down on a mouthful of flapjacks soaked in melted butter and maple syrup, Sean mumbled, "Mummph," and shook his head.

"You remember," Brian said. "We talked about the stolen horse. I said I thought it was probably hidden somewhere nearby and hasn't been taken away from the area yet."

Sean gave a gigantic gulp. "We weren't talking about the horse," he said impatiently. "You were doing all the talking, Brian. We're here to have fun at the dude ranch for two weeks, not to go searching for a stolen horse."

"Dad told me that a lot of his success comes from years of experience," Brian said, ignoring Sean's objections, "so it makes sense that I get in all the experience I can. A horse who's stolen and disappears is a perfect case to try to solve."

"Okay, okay," Sean said, "but you didn't bring your detecting stuff with you. You know, magnifying glass, flashlight, and whatever else you usually use."

"I brought it all," Brian said, "and I've already started making notes."

Sean groaned. When Brian was determined to solve a case, Sean knew it was a lot easier to just go along with him. At the very least, however, Sean decided he wouldn't have to solve the case on an empty stomach. "If you're not going to eat your flapjacks, I will."

"I'm going to eat them," Brian said, and deliberately took a large bite. "We can think and talk and eat at the same time, can't we?"

"You think and talk. I'll eat," Sean said. "Do you want that piece of bacon?"

"Be serious," Brian said. "Help me think about where the horse could be hidden."

"In a barn?" Sean said.

Brian shook his head. "Way too obvious," he said.

"Well," Sean joked. "How about in one of the other cabins?"

Brian rolled his eyes. "Very funny," he said. Then he had an idea. "How about in a cave?"

"Or a mine!" Sean said.

Brian thought it over. "It's possible. But which one? Mr. Austin said there were abandoned mines all over this part of Nevada."

Carter suddenly jumped out from behind the thick trunk of an oak tree. "So!" he said, pointing an accusing finger at Brian. "It's not just the mine you're after! You think you can find the stolen horse, too, and be a real hero, do you?"

Brian jumped to his feet. "You were spying on us!" he shouted angrily.

"It wouldn't be the first time," Sean said. "I was going to tell you, Brian, but I forgot. Carter was awake and listening in last night, too."

"So what if I was?" Carter said. "I know this countryside better than you two do," he bragged. "If anybody's going to find Nightstar, it's going to be me!"

"Keep your voice down," Brian said. "Do you

want to get us all in trouble?"

"You think you're such a hotshot just because your dad's a private investigator," Carter hissed. "But if that horse really is hidden around here, you're not going to find him! I am!"

"How?" Sean asked. "By getting lost again?"

Carter glared at Sean, then turned to Brian. "I'll find him," he said, "but since Hank insists on the buddy system, I'm willing to let you tag along with me. Just don't get in my way."

"Forget it," Brian said. "I've already got a buddy."

Carter's mouth turned down in a sneer. "Who? Vaughn?" He laughed meanly. "Okay, big investigator. You're about to lose a case!"

5

BOBBY WAS OUT OF BREATH as he ran up and plopped down next to Sean. "Aren't you through eating yet?" he asked. "Hurry up. We're going to ride along the east ridge trail."

Sean and Brian picked up their empty plates, utensils, and tin mugs and walked to the trail wagon, where the cleanup was taking place.

"Hurry up," Bobby insisted as Sean and Brian rejoined the group. Sean groaned. It looked like Bobby was back to sticking to him like glue.

"Let's go!" Mr. Austin called out after the boys had mounted their horses.

The trail led upward through the forest along a narrow ridge that wound back and forth across the mountain like a yellow ribbon. As the boys rode, the sun climbed higher, gleaming off the tops of the thickly clustered pines.

All Sean could see in any direction was forest. Except for a thin wisp of smoke from what Sean decided must be the lodge's chimney, there was no sign of the Austin Dude Ranch. Sean thought about the campfire tale of the lost mine and the dead prospector whose ghost never gave up haunting it. He wasn't surprised that the poor prospector couldn't find his mine if it was hidden somewhere in these mountains.

Soon the trail wound down along the opposite side of the mountain, and the riders emerged from the trees into a large clearing. Carter, riding just ahead of Brian, turned and called, "That's Wade Morrison's ranch. This trail divides his property from Hank Austin's."

Brian glanced across at the house and barns and fenced-in exercise fields, but his thoughts were interrupted as something flicked against his face: a peanut shell!

"Cut it out, Carter!" he called. "Stop throwing peanut shells!"

Carter just laughed, faced forward, and popped a handful of peanuts into his mouth.

Woody rode up beside Brian. "Anything wrong?" he asked.

Brian shook his head and said, "It's okay. I was just talking to Carter."

As Woody fell into place beside him, Brian asked, "What kind of horses do they keep on that ranch?"

"Horses used for working the ranch and horses used for breeding," Woody said.

Brian nodded. "Can you tell me about Nightstar?" he asked. "Was he Mr. Morrison's most valuable horse?"

"You'll have to ask somebody else your questions. That's Wade Morrison's business."

Brian tried again. "Do the Morrisons raise and sell many horses? I mean, it doesn't look like a very big ranch."

"I told you," snapped Woody, "if you want answers to all those questions, you'll have to ask Wade Morrison himself. I work on the Austin ranch and keep to myself. Nothing Mr. Morrison does is my business."

Brian was about to try asking one more question when Woody abruptly rode off.

A SHORT TIME LATER a husky, deeply tanned rider appeared from out of the woods and pulled his horse to a stop along the trail. He raised a hand in greeting, and Mr. Austin and some of the boys waved back.

Carter shouted, "Hi, Mr. Morrison!"

So that's Wade Morrison, Brian thought. He saw Mr. Morrison look right at Woody and say something to him. Woody looked angry. As Brian rode by, he could hear them arguing.

"You'll do what I say or else!" Mr. Morrison said. Then he turned and rode away.

For the rest of the ride Brian avoided Carter.

Later Brian joined Dan and some of the other boys watching a demonstration on calf roping.

"Where's your brother?" Dan asked Brian.

"He's helping brush down the horses, then he's going swimming."

Dan was perched on the top rail of the fence next to Brian. "I wonder what the statistics are," he said out of the blue.

"What statistics?"

"On how long it takes, on the average, from start to finish, to rope a calf. Then there's what percentage of calves get away," Dan continued matter-of-factly. "You know, stuff like that. If I could feed all the data into a computer, I could come up with a precise statistical profile."

"For just this ranch?" Brian teased. "Or the whole state of Nevada?"

Dan's eyes shone. "There's no limit. For the whole world!"

"Fascinating," Brian said.

"Yeah," Dan said dreamily. "I know."

"My father uses computers in his business as a private investigator," Brian told Dan.

Dan turned to study Brian. "How?" he asked.

"Computer searches," Brian said.

Dan gave a nod of approval. "That's very interesting," he told Brian. "Do you know that, someday, everything it's possible to know about everyone will be on computer?"

"Not about me it won't!" The boys both turned and saw Cookie. He leaned on the fence next to them. "Anybody wants to know about me, they can just step up and ask."

"Actually," Brian said, "I've got a question. But it's not about you. It's about the horse stolen from the Morrison ranch."

Now it was Cookie's turn to look surprised. "Well," he said, scratching his head, "Nightstar ain't exactly a specialty of mine, but I'll tell you what I can."

"Is losing Nightstar going to hurt Mr. Morrison's business?" asked Brian. "Nightstar was a valuable piece of property."

"I'm sure he feels real bad about losing the horse," Cookie said, "but an animal like that is always insured. He may not get Nightstar back, but he'll get reimbursed for some of his worth."

As they talked, a tall ranch hand named Will, who had been standing nearby, walked over. "It ain't as if Morrison ain't had trouble enough without losing his most valuable horse," he said.

"What kind of trouble?" asked Brian.

"Some of the colts Nightstar sired over the past three years are developing weak ankles," said Will. "I heard that at least one customer's been giving Morrison a real bad time about it."

"Why blame Nightstar?" Brian asked. "He was a racehorse. He couldn't have had weak ankles."

Will shrugged. "That's the funny thing," he said. "The weakness didn't come from the mares. That much I'm sure of."

Brian had pulled out his notebook. "How can you be so sure?" he asked Will.

"By checking the mare's lineage," Will explained.

"What about Nightstar's lineage?" Brian asked. "And what about the colts he sired earlier?"

"Never heard of any problems with either," Will said.

"Are you sure?" Brian asked.

"As sure as the sun sets in the west," Will said. He told Brian he had work to do, and Brian thanked him as he walked away.

Brian said to Cookie, "I've got one more question. Mr. Morrison came up while we were riding by and waved to us. He said something to Woody, but Woody wouldn't even look at him."

Cookie shook his head. "All I know is there's some kind of bad feeling between the two of them, stemming from when Woody used to work for Morrison on his ranch."

"He worked for him?" asked Brian, surprised. "How long ago was that?"

"Woody was there for a number of years,"

Cookie said. "They were good friends, even. When Woody needed money to buy his own ranch, Wade Morrison loaned him the money to get started. It didn't work out, though. Woody didn't have much of a head for business. Even so, Woody was one of the few people Mr. Morrison ever trusted around Nightstar." He shook his head. "Then three years or so ago Morrison and Woody had some angry words."

"About what?" asked Brian.

"I'm not sure," Cookie said. "Woody pretty much keeps his thoughts to himself."

"Was he fired?" Brian asked. "Or did he quit?"

"I don't know that neither," Cookie said, "but he left Morrison and came to work for Mr. Austin."

Cookie sauntered off to talk to some of the other boys, and Brian went carefully over his notes. Now he was even more puzzled about Woody.

"You think Woody has something to do with

the disappearance of Nightstar?" Dan asked.

"It's possible," Brian said. He tucked his notebook back into his pocket and leaned on the rail again.

"A few minutes ago we were talking about computer searches," he told Dan. "How'd you like to help me do one right now?"

Dan's eyes lit up. "Sure!" Then he groaned and made a face. "I can't. I promised my parents I wouldn't touch a computer while I was here, remember?"

"You don't have to touch it," Brian answered slyly. Dan gave him a quizzical glance. "I'll do that part," Brian explained.

"What do you want to look up?" Dan inquired.

"Nightstar's lineage," Brian said.

Dan whistled. "How about something easy?"

"There have to be records somewhere. Want to try?"

It took Dan only a second to make up his mind. "Let's go!" he said.

6

BRIAN KNOCKED on the office door and waited. "Cool," he told Dan after a few minutes. "Nobody's home."

Dan nudged Brian. Through the window he could see a computer on a desk.

Brian opened the door, and they tiptoed in. The office appeared deserted.

"Maybe we should ask permission to use it," Dan said.

"There's no one here to ask," Brian pointed out. "Besides, Mrs. Austin said she was here to answer any question we might have, right? Well, I have a question only her computer can answer."

"Right," agreed Dan.

Brian sat down at the computer and flipped the

switch that turned it on. Dan bent over his shoulder, his eyes on the screen, and they waited impatiently until the menu came up.

"Press CODE and F3 to get the directory," Dan said.

Brian did, and Dan studied it. "There," he said and pointed to a listing of STOCK. "Try that. Press EXIT and get back to REVISE DOCUMENT."

As Brian followed directions, Dan said, "Type in STOCK. When it comes up press FIND. Then type in NIGHTSTAR."

Brian did, but the message appeared on the screen: "NIGHTSTAR not found."

Dan frowned. "They don't have a modem," he said. "They're not hooked into any of the programs. If they were, I could probably hack into Mr. Morrison's computer, figure out his code, and check his records."

"I need to know more about what kind of information's kept on a horse," Brian said. "I'm going to try THUNDER. That's one of the

Austins' horses."

The computer brought up THUNDER along with a couple of paragraphs of information. Some of it was abbreviated, but Brian could figure it out.

"Here's his parents and grandparents," Brian said, pointing. "And here is the location and date of birth. Here's some other dates, whatever they mean. But what's this string of numbers?"

"I don't know," Dan said.

Brian scrolled back a page to a listing for another horse. "Here's GOLDIE. Hey, look! Here's another string of numbers."

Mrs. Austin burst into the office.

"What are you boys doing?" she demanded.

Brian and Dan froze. She didn't look nearly as friendly as she had the evening before.

"We were going to ask permission," Brian said, "but nobody was here."

"The offices are out-of-bounds," Mrs. Austin said sternly.

"We didn't know," Dan said, improvising. "It's not in the rules."

Mrs. Austin folded her arms and sighed. Brian thought she looked a bit less angry. "In the meantime, suppose you answer my question and tell me what you're doing."

"We wanted to see what kind of records are kept on a horse."

"What on earth for?" she asked.

Brian explained.

"So you're the one my husband told me about," she said. "The boy with a million questions. Very well, what can I do to help?"

Brian smiled and pointed at the screen. "Is this an identification number for the horse?"

"Yes, that's exactly what it is."

"Does every horse have one?" asked Brian.

"Every registered horse does."

"Are the numbers listed anywhere else besides in a rancher's records?"

"Yes, the number is listed with a particular

group, such as the Racehorse Club Association or the Horses of the Americas Registry. All the groups are listed in the National Encyclopedia of Associations. And the identification number is also tattooed inside the horse's lower lip."

"Do most ranch owners keep this kind of computer information about their horses?" Brian asked.

"We all keep records, and nowadays most are on computers. Which horse are you trying to look up?" she asked.

"Nightstar," Brian said.

Mrs. Austin's eyes widened. "Nightstar's Mr. Morrison's horse. He's not one of ours. You know, don't you, that Nightstar was stolen?"

Brian nodded and said, "That's what made me curious about him." He went on to explain what he had learned so far and why he had accessed the computer. Mrs. Austin actually seemed impressed.

"Turn off the computer and come with me,"

Mrs. Austin said. "I've got something that might be of interest to you."

The boys followed Mrs. Austin into another room and waited as she reached into a bookcase on the back wall, pulled out a book, and opened it on the desk.

"Here he is," Mrs. Austin said, pointing to a picture of a beautiful coal black horse. Brian and Dan leaned over her shoulder and read about Nightstar. Brian pulled out his notebook and jotted down some information from the entry.

"Do you know if the police have Nightstar's ID number?" Brian asked.

"I can't imagine why they wouldn't," she said, closing the book and getting up to put it back on the shelf. "When a horse is stolen, the identification number is one of the first things the police ask for."

"Thanks, Mrs. Austin," Brian said. "That information was very helpful.

"And thanks for not yelling at us about the

computer," he added.

Mrs. Austin laughed. "You're welcome," she said. "Just keep in mind that from now on the offices are out-of-bounds."

Brian and Dan promised her they would remember, and left. "I'm sorry I couldn't access Mr. Morrison's computer for you," Dan told Brian as they walked along the path back to their cabin.

"It's okay," Brian said. "You heard what Mrs. Austin said. There are other places to get Night-star's ID number."

"Now what are you going to do?"

"I'm going to try to find out how much Nightstar was insured for," Brian answered.

"How are you going to do that?"

"There was a name of an insurance company listed with Thunder's information. I'll take a chance that Mr. Morrison used the same company to insure his horses."

"What if he didn't?" Dan asked.

"One step at a time," Brian said. He fished in

the pockets of his jeans and came up empty. "Have you got a quarter I can borrow?"

Dan handed Brian a quarter, and they headed for the pay phone outside the lodge. Brian thumbed through the phone book, found the listing for the insurance company, dropped his quarter into the phone, and dialed the number.

"But you're just a kid," Dan interrupted. "Whoever answers will just think you're some jerk playing a prank."

Brian smiled and mouthed a silent "Watch this."

When a receptionist answered, deepened his voice. It was so realistic that Dan had a hard time not laughing.

"I'm investigating the disappearance of Wade Morrison's horse Nightstar," Brian said. "Am I correct in assuming he's insured by your company?"

"The sheriff has already been here to talk to us," the receptionist answered impatiently. "Oh well, wait a minute. I'll connect you with one of our agents."

"Looks good," Brian excitedly whispered to Dan, cupping his hand over the mouthpiece. "This must be the company or the sheriff wouldn't have been there asking questions."

When the agent came on the line Brian identified himself as a detective following up on information on the disappearance of Nightstar.

"There's nothing more I can tell you," the agent answered wearily. "Mr. Morrison hasn't filed a claim as yet. Until he does, there's nothing we can do."

"Can you tell me how much Nightstar's insured for?"

"Your department already has that information. Just who did you say you are?" the agent suddenly asked.

"Thanks for your help," Brian said quickly, and hung up.

"Whoa!" said Dan. "That was incredible. You had that guy totally fooled."

"Not totally," Brian said, frowning. "He wouldn't tell me how much Nightstar is insured for, just that Mr. Morrison hasn't filed a claim yet."

"So what do you do now?" Dan asked.

"I don't know," Brian told him. "I have to think about it."

The boys spent the rest of the day swimming, riding, and hiking. Brian was so busy with one activity after another he didn't have time to think about Nightstar. And that evening after a huge supper, the staff organized a no-talent show that kept everybody laughing. Brian was so tired that night he was asleep almost before his head hit the pillow.

THE NEXT DAY just before lunch, Brian sat down on the bench in front of the lodge and reviewed the notes he had made in his notebook. After a few minutes he frowned. His father had taught him that in building a case, start with what you know first. But all Brian really had so far were questions. Lots of questions. For instance, What would make Mr. Morrison delay in filing an insurance claim? And what did Woody know about Nightstar? When Woody stopped working for Mr. Morrison, could his reasons have had anything to do with the missing horse? And what could Mr. Morrison have meant when he warned Woody "or else"? Or else what?

Suddenly a hissing voice startled him. "Ssst!" Sean stepped out from behind a tree. "Brian" he asked, "Bobby isn't around somewhere, is he?"

"No, he isn't," Brian said. "What's the problem, Sean?"

Sean carefully looked to both sides before he sneaked out from his hiding place.

"Bobby's a nice guy," Sean explained, "but he sticks to me like glue." He pulled a wad of string from his pocket. "Now he wants me to help him make a kite."

Just then they saw Will walking hurriedly down the path toward them. "Either of you boys seen

Carter lately?" he called out.

"I haven't seen him since breakfast," Brian answered.

"Me, either," Sean said. "But he's got to be somewhere around here. Right?"

"That's what we're trying to find out," Will said. "Mike showed us where he saw Carter take off by himself into the woods behind the cabins. That was a few hours ago, and no one has seen him since. Mr. Austin and some of the others are already out looking for him. If you see Carter, let me know right away."

As soon as Will left, Sean asked, "Brian, do you suppose Carter really meant what he told us? Do you think he went looking for the stolen horse?" Sean began to get that creepy feeling he always felt when he thought something bad was going to happen.

"He got in big trouble before when he broke the rules and went off by himself," Brian said. "He wouldn't do it again."

"He wouldn't? Then why can't anyone find him?"

Brian wondered if he should have paid more attention to Carter's bragging. "He did say he was going to find the missing horse before we did."

"We'd better tell Mr. Austin," Sean said. His stomach was really beginning to hurt.

"Will said he and the others already went looking for Carter," Brian said.

"You're right," Sean said. "What about Will? Should we tell him what we know?"

"All we know is what Will already knows," Brian said. "That Carter wandered off and is missing."

"Yeah," Sean said, "but wandered off where?"

Brian jumped up and walked quickly toward the cabin. "That's what we're going to find out!" he called back over his shoulder.

"Really?" Sean glanced at the heavy forest surrounding the camp and sighed. "Just how are we going to do that?"

7

"SEAN!" Bobby yelled from the lodge porch. "Hey, Sean!" He jumped down the stairs and ran up to Brian and Sean.

"You didn't come in for lunch," he complained to Sean. "I was waiting for you. I even saved you a seat."

"Go back and eat," Sean answered. "I'm going to skip lunch. There's something Brian and I have to do."

"What?" Bobby asked excitedly. "I'll do it with you."

"No, you won't." Sean was already worried enough about how they'd find Carter. He didn't want to have to worry about Bobby, too. He took Bobby by the shoulders and turned him back toward the lodge. "Go in and finish your lunch,"

Sean told him. "I'll be back as soon as I can."

"You promise?" Bobby asked, and Sean nodded. Bobby walked away.

Sean looked at Brian, who was smiling. "What's so funny?" Sean asked.

"Bobby is more in love with you than your girlfriend, Debbie Jean Parker, is."

Sean flared red with embarrassment. "Debbie Jean Parker is not my girlfriend!" he shouted, but Brian had already walked to the edge of the clearing and was bent down examining the ground.

"When Carter got lost before," Brian said, "he was following Woody and looking for Deadman's Mine. My guess is that he'll take the same route."

"Not so loud," Sean said. "Bobby's still close enough to hear."

Brian lowered his voice. "Mike said that Carter entered the woods behind the cabins. All we have to do is pick up his trail."

"His trail?" asked Sean. "Why are you so sure

we can follow his trail?"

Brian smiled. "Since we've been here Carter hasn't once been without a bag of peanuts. I'm hoping he'll be as messy on the trail as he is in camp."

"You mean we're going to follow his trail of peanut shells?" Sean asked.

"Right."

"Won't the people who are looking for him notice the peanut shells?"

"I don't think so," Brian said. "Maybe there won't even be any peanut shells, or not enough to follow, but we can look for them."

Brian and Sean walked along the edge of the clearing, searching the ground.

Heavy boot prints were visible in the soft earth. "Here's where the searchers entered the forest," Brian said. "It's probably the place Mike pointed out to Will." He listened carefully. "I can't hear anyone in the forest. They must be quite a ways ahead of us."

"Look!" Sean said. He pried up a peanut shell where it had been tramped into the soft ground.

"Here's another shell . . . and another." Brian pointed at a scattering of peanut shells.

"I don't think the searchers were following the shells or they wouldn't have stepped on them," Sean said.

"There's only one way to find out," Brian said. "Let's go."

They followed the trail of shells into the forest.

"Here's another one!" Sean called out. "And there's one over here!" Sean chuckled. "I feel like Hansel and Gretel."

Brian pulled his knife from his pocket. "Hansel and Gretel made a trail, and we'll make one, too. I brought along my compass, but it will be easier to find our way back if we've clearly marked our trail. Give me the string you've got in your pocket."

Brian cut a six-inch length of the kite string and tied it to the end of a low branch. He cut the rest of the string into pieces and began tying them to branches as they walked deeper and deeper into the woods.

Even with the sun high overhead, the woods were dim, shadowy, and eerily quiet. A soft blanket of pine needles carpeted the ground, but an occasional twig snapped loudly beneath their feet. Now and then Brian and Sean heard strange rustling sounds nearby. But they didn't hear voices or sounds that might be the searchers.

"I don't see any signs that the searchers came this way," Sean said.

"I don't, either," Brian told him. "They must have taken a different direction somewhere back there."

Sean flopped onto the ground. "It's all uphill, and I'm tired," he said. "Can we rest for a couple of minutes?"

"Sure," Brian said, and he sat down next to Sean.

A twig snapped. "What was that?" Sean asked,

looking behind him into the tangled brush.

"It might have been an animal," Brian said.

"What kind of animal?" asked Sean. "A mountain lion? A bear?"

"Not this close to the ranches," Brian said. "What we probably heard was a rabbit or a wood rat, or something like that."

"Rats?" said Sean. "Yuck! I hate rats!"

Suddenly there was a loud crash, and Sean whirled and screamed as something came bounding out of the brush.

"Bobby!" Sean said, groaning. "I told you to stay at the lodge!"

"I don't have to do what you say," Bobby said. "You're not my mother. Besides, if you didn't want anyone to follow you, you shouldn't have left a trail." Bobby grinned and held up a fistful of string.

"Bobby!" Brian complained. "The pieces of string were there to make it easy to find our way back!"

"Oh," Bobby said. "Well, maybe Woody will help us."

"Woody?" Brian said. "What does Woody have to do with this?"

"When Mr. Austin went with some of the others to search for Carter, he left Woody in charge. I wanted to help, too, so I told Woody what I heard you say about Carter and that you and Sean were going to go look for him."

"What did Woody do then?" Brian asked.

Bobby shrugged. "He went into the office and made some phone calls."

Bobby looked at Brian, then at Sean. "So, where's Carter?" he asked.

8

THE CLIMB WAS STEEP and very hot, but every now and then Bobby, Sean, and Brian spotted a discarded peanut shell or two, so they kept on.

"How far did Carter go?" Sean grumbled.

"I don't know," Brian said, wiping his face with his shirtsleeve. "I'm guessing that by now we've left the Austin property and are on the Morrison ranch."

At that point the trail of peanut shells led upward onto a wide rock ledge edged on one side with a thick tangle of dead branches and underbrush.

"You need a machete to cut through this junk," Brian complained as they began pushing branches out of the way.

"Just like your room at home," Sean joked.

"Very funny," said Brian.

"I see two peanut shells," Bobby called out, and pointed. "And there's another one farther up."

Sean started toward Bobby. But suddenly Brian stopped.

"Wait a minute, Sean," he said. "What would a pile of dead branches be doing on a rock ledge in the middle of a forest?"

Sean shrugged uncomprehendingly. "I guess it was easier than carting the branches to the middle of someplace else," Sean answered.

"Sean!" Brian said. "Think! Remember what Cookie said about a rock ledge and what Woody said about the brush covering the doorway to the mine?"

Suddenly Sean remembered. He grinned. "Right. And this has got to be the highest peak around here!"

Brian glanced at the sun. "And we're facing south."

Brian and Sean frantically began pulling away the tangle of branches.

"I knew it!" Brian said when they discovered a wooden door frame in the wall of the ledge. "It's the entrance to Deadman's Mine! It's real!"

Brian heaved open the door.

"L-look!" Sean shouted.

Bobby let out a yell and grabbed Sean's arm.

"Th-the p-prospector's skeleton!" Sean screamed.

Facing them was a dusty skeleton, its nearly toothless skull grinning a welcome.

"Brian! The prospector's skeleton is here, just like Woody said! This has to be the lost Deadman's Mine! We found it! We really found it!"

"We sure did!" said Brian. "Let's check it out."

A section of a once shored-up ceiling had collapsed at one side of the large, dug-out space just inside the door, letting in sunlight.

"That's funny," Brian said as they looked around inside the mine.

"What?" asked Sean.

"This mine was supposed to be abandoned. But everything looks too neat." Brian pointed. "Look."

Rotted, fallen timbers had been cleared and piled next to a stack of old boxes and tools.

"You're right," said Sean. "That is weird."

"Peeuuu!" said Bobby as he pinched his nose closed. "What's that stink?"

Brian sniffed. So did Sean.

"I know that smell," Sean said. He and Brian grinned.

"Horses!"

Brian carefully crossed the open space of the mine to where it made a turn to the left. Sean and Bobby followed him closely.

A large black horse, tethered to a wooden post, whinnied as Brian approached.

"You were right, Sean," said Brian. "A mine was the perfect place to hide a stolen horse."

The horse's right front ankle was tightly wrapped, and it favored that leg, limping a little as it nervously backed away from Brian.

"Nightstar!" Brian said, instantly recognizing him from the photos in Mrs. Austin's book.

Sean stared at the horse. "Excellent," he said. "But what do we do now? Try to return the horse or keep looking for Carter?"

"I want to check something," Brian said. He pulled his notebook and pen from his pocket and handed them to Sean. "I'm going to give you a number. Write it down."

Sean took them and watched Brian slowly approach the horse. "What are you going to do?"

"Look inside his lower lip for an identification number that's tattooed there."

"Yikes! What if he bites?"

Brian had wondered the same thing, but he hoped that horses were like dogs and behaved well with people who didn't seem afraid of them. He gently stroked the horse's neck and nose while he murmured, "Good boy, Night-star. I won't hurt you."

He pulled down the horse's lower lip and read the number to Sean. Nightstar whinnied and pulled away, and Brian jumped back quickly, afraid the horse might step on his feet.

"Sean!" he said suddenly, looking at his hands. He showed them to Sean. Both palms were smeared with black dye. "Do you know what this means?"

But Bobby interrupted by whimpering, "I don't like it in here, you guys. Let's go back to the ranch."

Just then a couple of loose stones rolled down from the entrance to the mine. Then came a spine-chilling wail.

"It's the ghost!" Sean shouted. "Let's get out of here!"

Brian grabbed his arm. "It's not a ghost! Watch out!" He pulled Sean out of the way as Carter came tumbling head over heels into the mine.

Carter sat up and stared at Brian. "What are you guys doing here?"

"Looking for you," Brian said.

Carter's eyes widened when he saw the horse. He glanced around, and Brian could see that he was finally beginning to figure things out.

"Hey! How about that? I found the lost mine!" Carter exclaimed. "And Nightstar! That's got to be Nightstar! I wonder if there's a reward!"

"You found them?" Sean said. "What do you think we're doing here?"

"We followed the trail of your peanut shells," Brian told Carter. "They led right past the mine and up the side of the mountain."

"Where you got lost," Bobby added.

Carter's face turned red. He was about to object when Brian said, "We can't stay here. We've got to take the horse back. We've got to call the sheriff."

"Before someone else gets here," Sean said.

"Someone else?" Bobby asked. "Like who?"

Sean froze when he heard a noise outside on the rock ledge. "Listen!" he whispered.

The sound came closer.

"Footsteps!" Brian said. "Look!"

A tall, heavyset figure stood menacingly in the doorway.

Sean gulped and nudged Brian. "Now what?" Sean asked in an alarmed tone.

Brian shook his head. "We're trapped."

9

"WHAT ARE YOU KIDS doing here?" the man demanded angrily.

"Mr. Morrison!" Carter yelled. "Boy, are we ever glad to see you!"

Mr. Morrison ignored Carter as he stepped into the mine. His face was red and sweaty, and Brian thought he appeared nervous.

Carter didn't seem to notice. "Hey, Mr. Morrison," he said, "we found Nightstar. Is there a reward? There ought to be."

"Be quiet, Carter," Brian mumbled.

"What for?" Carter told Brian. "I found Nightstar and I want my reward. Isn't that right, Mr. Morrison?"

"Shut up," hissed Brian.

Mr. Morrison shot Brian a look, then smiled. "You best listen to your little friend," Mr. Morrison told Carter in a menacing tone. "Before your big mouth gets you into a heap of real trouble."

Carter was confused. "What are you talking about, Mr. Morrison? I found Nightstar. He's right there." Carter pointed to the horse.

Mr. Morrison gave a mirthless laugh. "I appreciate you boys locating my horse, but I'm afraid the only reward you'll be collecting will be six feet under."

Bobby took a few steps back. "What is he talking about?" he asked Brian nervously.

"What's going on?" asked Carter as Mr. Morrison slid a knife out from a sheath at his belt and stepped toward him. "Hey, you guys!" screamed Carter. "Help!"

Just then Brian sprang at Mr. Morrison, knocking him backward. "Run!" Brian yelled, but before any of them could get away, Mr. Morrison quickly scrambled to his feet, the knife blade flashing in his hand.

"You snooping kids have been nothing but trouble from the beginning," he growled. "But now I'm going to take care of all of you once and for all!"

"Hold it right there!"

Mr. Morrison whirled, and standing at the entrance of the cave were Woody and the local sheriff. The sheriff had his gun drawn and aimed at Mr. Morrison.

"It's over, Morrison," he said. "Drop the knife."

"Drop it, Wade," Woody said. "He's right. It's over."

Mr. Morrison took a long look at Woody. "I told you to keep your mouth shut," he told him, but Woody just shook his head and shrugged.

"I couldn't keep your secret no more, Wade," he said.

"You're a fool, Woody," said Mr. Morrison, and he let the knife fall to the dirt. The sheriff immediately grabbed his arms and clicked a pair of handcuffs on his wrists.

"What's going on?" Sean asked.

"Yeah," grumbled Carter. "And what secret is Woody talking about?"

The sheriff turned to Brian and smiled. "If I'm right, you must be the young man who's been asking all the questions about Nightstar."

"Yes, sir," Brian said.

The sheriff nodded. "I'm Sheriff Anderson," he said. "Your friend Woody here called me not too long ago and said some kid detective was about to crack the case about the disappearance of Nightstar."

The boys all looked at Brian, who sensed from their confused expressions that they expected some kind of explanation.

"Well," Brian said, "three years ago Woody and Mr. Morrison had a falling out."

"Over what?" Sean asked.

"Nightstar," Brian said. "I'm guessing that he died. But since Mr. Morrison didn't want to lose his high breeding fees, he decided to substitute another horse who looked just like Nightstar." Brian held up his dye-streaked hands. "Or pretty close, anyway. If you really look, you can see the spots on this horse. He's not Nightstar."

"Wow," said Sean.

"Yeah," said Brian, "but Woody found out about it. That's what their big fight was all about."

Woody nodded his head.

"But Mr. Morrison was getting in big trouble lately because some of the horse's colts began to develop serious ankle problems. He knew that an investigation would expose his fraud, so he pressured Woody into helping him."

"That's why after Nightstar was stolen he never filed an insurance claim!" said Sean, remembering what Brian had told him.

"Right," said Brian.

"But how did he pressure Woody?" asked Carter.

"Cookie told me that Woody had borrowed a

lot of money from Morrison to buy a ranch. When the ranch failed, Woody couldn't pay it back. I bet Morrison told Woody that if he helped keep the fraud quiet, he would forgive the loan."

"Cool, Brian! You cracked the case," Sean said, and gave him a high five.

"We all helped solve the case," Brian said. "Even Carter."

"Really?" asked Carter.

"Sure," said Brian. "You see, when Woody found out that you were determined to locate Deadman's Mine, he decided to put the skeleton at the entrance to scare you away, at least until he could find someplace new to hide the horse."

"What happened?" Carter asked.

"He realized it was only a matter of time before you found it. I think that's why he made those phone calls. He was worried that someone might actually get hurt in the mine. He couldn't let that happen."

"Is that right, Woody?" Carter asked.

Woody nodded. "Yeah. I got to thinking about what might happen if one of you boys stumbled into a mine and got hurt." He shook his head. "It just wasn't worth it. So I called Morrison and told him I'd had enough. I was turning myself in. That's when I called the sheriff here."

"And it's a darn good thing we got here when we did," Sheriff Anderson said. "You boys are lucky you weren't seriously hurt."

"You're right, sir," Brian said, and the boys all mumbled their apologies.

The sheriff smiled and tipped his hat. "I best bring this one down to jail," he said, pushing Morrison ahead of him. "Woody," he said, "I trust you to turn yourself in this afternoon like we planned?"

"I'll be there," he said. The sheriff left with Morrison, then Woody took the reins of the horse and led him out of the cave. At the entrance he turned around. "I'm really sorry I didn't tell the truth sooner. But thanks."

The boys waved good-bye to Woody, then they all sighed with relief.

Brian walked over to Carter. "What do you say we be friends?" He held out his hand, and Carter smiled and shook hands.

"Cool," he said.

The boys all laughed.

"Gee," Bobby said at last, "I'm actually kind of sorry to find out that there really is no such thing as Deadman's Mine."

"Yeah," said Sean. "Me, too. It was fun."

All of a sudden, from somewhere deep inside the dark mine came an eerie grumbling.

"What was that?" asked Bobby nervously, just as a rush of cold air brushed their faces. A low moan echoed through the mine, followed by what sounded like the rattling of chains.

The boys all turned to one another—eyes as

wide as saucers. "The prospector's ghost!" they screamed, and ran as fast as they could. Even so, Sean couldn't help but laugh at a thought he couldn't get out of his head: Just wait until Sam Miyako hears about this!

JOAN LOWERY NIXON is a renowned writer of children's mysteries. She is the author of more than eighty books and the only four-time recipient of the prestigious Edgar Allan Poe Award for the best juvenile mystery of the year.

❰

"I was asked by Disney Adventures *magazine if I could write a short mystery. I decided to write about two young boys who help their father, a private investigator, solve crimes. These boys, Brian and Sean, are actually based on my grandchildren, who are the same ages as the characters. My first Casebusters story was a piece about a ghost that haunts an inn. This derives from a legendary Louisiana inn I visited which was allegedly haunted. Later, I learned the owner had made up the entire tale, and I used that angle in the story."*

— JOAN LOWERY NIXON